This book belongs to

. . . .

Published by Ladybird Books Ltd 2012
A Penguin Company
Penguin Books Ltd, 80 Strand, London, WC2R ORL, UK
Penguin Books Australia Ltd, 707 Collins Street, Melbourne, Victoria 3008, Australia
Penguin Books (NZ), 67 Apollo Drive, Rosedale, Auckland
0632, New Zealand (a divison of Pearson New Zealand Ltd)

www.ladybird.com

ISBN 978 -1- 40931- 321-2

013

Printed in China

This book is based on the
TV Series 'Peppa Pig'
'Peppa Pig' is created by
Neville Astley and Mark Baker

www.peppapig.com

The BIGGEST Muddy Puddle in the World

Once upon a time, Mummy Pig and Daddy Pig were tucking Peppa and George into bed.

"There's so much rain!" Peppa said.

"That means there will be muddy puddles to jump in tomorrow," Mummy Pig smiled.

The splish-splash-splosh of raindrops on the window sang Peppa and George to sleep, dreaming of muddy puddles.

While Peppa and George slept, it rained.

And rained.

And rained.

It rained so much that the next morning, when Daddy Pig ran out to jump in a muddy puddle, he landed straight in a massive pool of water! "Oh! Who put all this water here?" Daddy Pig said as he swam back to the house. "And where are the muddy puddles?" asked Peppa.

“Our house is like a desert island!” Peppa laughed, looking at all the water.

“Oh dear,” Mummy Pig said. “How will we get our food?”

Granny Pig and Grandpa Pig arrived on their boat. "Ahoy, there!" Grandpa Pig said. "Wonderful boating weather!"
"Do you need anything from the shop?" Granny Pig asked.
"Can we come too?" Peppa said.
"Yes! Then you can help us get shopping for *everybody*!"

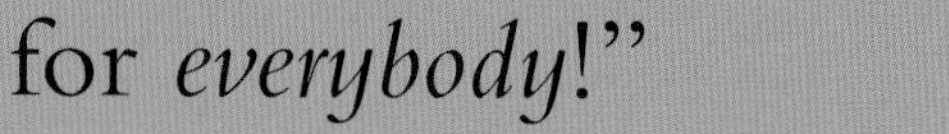

"Polly can be our shopping list. She's very good at remembering things," Granny Pig said, beaming at Polly. "Who's a clever parrot?"

"Squawk! Who's a clever parrot?" Polly copied. Polly was good at copying what people said!

Peppa, George, Grandpa Pig, Granny Pig and Polly Parrot sailed across the water. It was almost as fun as jumping in a muddy puddle.

Each house was like its own desert island.
They sailed from house to boat to submarine,
asking if people needed anything from the shop.

“Do you need anything from the shop?”

“Chocolate, please,” Suzy Sheep said.
“Squawk! Chocolate!” Polly Parrot copied.

"A newspaper and a comic, please," Granddad Dog and Danny Dog said.
"Squawk! Newspaper! Comic!" Polly Parrot copied.

"Cheese, please," Grampy Rabbit said.
"Squawk! Cheese!" Polly Parrot copied.

When Grandpa Pig's boat arrived at the supermarket, Miss Rabbit was all alone. "Silly, isn't it? A little bit of rain and everyone stays at home. What can I get you?"
"Polly has a list," Peppa said proudly.

Polly Parrot opened her beak and said,
"Who's a clever parrot? Who's a clever parrot?"
Oh dear. Polly Parrot had forgotten the list!

Luckily, Peppa remembered what everyone wanted! Grandpa Pig sailed back from submarine to boat to house.

"Cheese!" Peppa said.
"Thank you, Peppa!" Grampy Rabbit said.

"Newspaper and comic!" Peppa said.
"Thanks, Peppa!" Granddad Dog and Danny Dog said.

"It was lucky Peppa was going to the shops," said Mummy Sheep. "Or else we'd have nothing for dinner."
"Here's your chocolate, Suzy!" Peppa said.
"Oh," said Mummy Sheep.

Peppa and George arrived back home in the evening.
"Did you have fun sailing with Grandpa?" Mummy Pig asked.
"Yes! I remembered what everyone wanted," Peppa yawned.
"But there were no muddy puddles."
George snorted in agreement.
"Maybe there will be some muddy puddles tomorrow," Daddy Pig said.

The next morning, the sun was shining brightly in the clear blue sky. Polly Parrot flew with a sprig of leaves in her beak to show them all that the water had gone. She landed on Grandpa Pig's boat that was now stuck on Peppa's front lawn!

“Oh!” Granny Pig said, looking out from the boat. “I wonder what kind of mess the flood has left.”

And what did they see? . . .

The houses that were once desert islands were now back to normal, sitting on top of their hills. The water that Peppa and George sailed through was now gone. And instead, at the bottom of Peppa and George's hill, was . . .

Squelch!
Hee!
Hee!

the biggest muddy puddle . . .

Hee! Hee!

Squelch!

in the
world!